SHINE OF THE MOON
METAMORPHOSIS

I WAS FOOLISH MY LOVE, I WAS SO CONCERNED THOU WOULD SLIP INTO DEATHS DEMESNE I THOUGHT NOT ON HOW IT WOULD BE IN A TIN MAN'S BODY
DON'T BE SILLY SHINE, YOU DID AN AMAZING THING IN BRINGING ME BACK, IT'S FINE, I'M SO SO GRATEFUL, I WILL GET USED TO THIS NEW FORM

NO! I CAN DO MORE, I WILL GET THEE A LIVING BODY

BUT YOU CAN'T, THAT WOULD MEAN KILLING ANOTHER PERSON
I HAVE ALREADY BEEN THROUGH THIS WITH NURLIN, NO, WE WON'T KILL SOMEONE BUT THERE MUST BE A WAY TO MAKE THEE A REAL PERSON AGAIN, AND SHH, THOU HAS NO SAY IN THIS – THIS I WILL DO!
FIRST, LET US GO TO VISIT THE WIZARD

I KNOW NOT WHY THOU PUT ON THY BACK AND LEG CLOTHS, THOU WILT NOT RUST
I KNOW IT'S SILLY BUT IT MAKES ME FEEL MORE NORMAL
WELL LET US HOPE THE WIZARD CAN HELP US

THE WIZARD LIVES ATOP THIS MOUNTAIN
MISS SHINE, DID YOU REALLY TRY TO GO ON AN ANOTHER ADVENTURE WITHOUT ME COMING ALONG?
NURLIN?

THE WIZARD SETS OBSTACLES AND TRAPS SO WARD THY FOOTSTEPS
THAT FLIMSY TWIG MAY TAKE YOU AND DALE BUT NOT ME I'M AFRAID

GREETINGS WIZARD, WE SEEK THY COUNCIL
WHY DO I EVEN BOTHER MAKING IT HARD TO GET HERE – WHAT DO YOU WANT GOBLIN, I DID WHAT YOU WANTED

THOU HAST MY THANKS FOR SAVING DALE, BUT NOW I SEEK A WAY TO MAKE HIM HUMAN AGAIN
NO! IT CAN'T BE DONE!

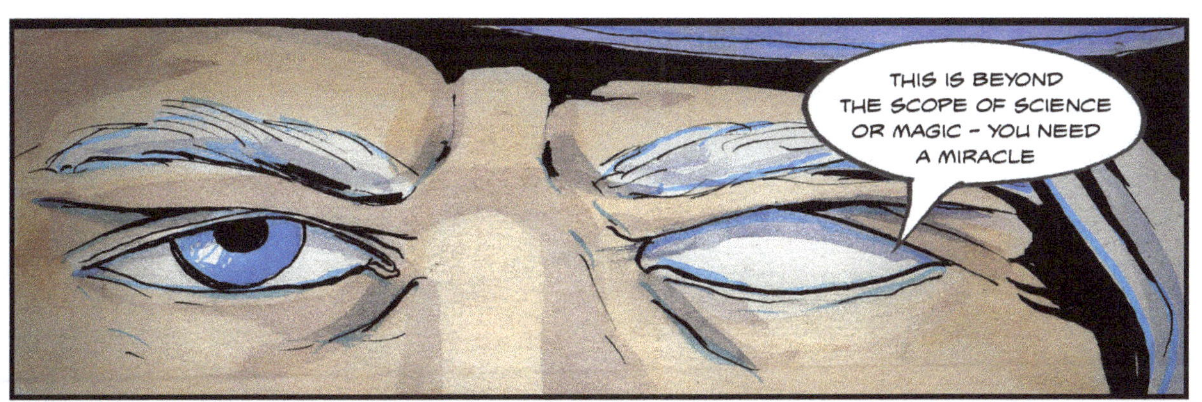

THIS IS BEYOND THE SCOPE OF SCIENCE OR MAGIC – YOU NEED A MIRACLE

WHAT DOST THOU MEAN – A MIRACLE?
WHAT YOU'RE TALKING ABOUT IS THE CREATION OF LIFE– THAT'S A HOLY MIRACLE! ONLY GODS CAN DO THAT! 
OK SO WE NEED A GOD TO HELP US WITH THIS. LET ME THINK... NOT PAN, HE IS THE REASON DALE LOST HIS BODY IN THE FIRST PLACE. THE ONLY OTHER GOD I KNOW IS JEHOVAH. HE'LL NOT HELP EITHER, LAST TIME I SAW HIM I PUNCHED HIM, HE LIKES ME NOT, BESIDE, HE IS A POOR, WEAK GOD HE IS FULL OF PROMISES BUT DOES NOTHING...
THEY HAVE SOME STRANGE GODS OVER IN QUEEN MAUDE'S LAND THEY SAY
IT'S OKAY SHINE, THIS BODY IS GREAT

LET US SEEK OUT SOME OF THESE GODS
IF WE CLIMB THE NEXT PEAK, WE CAN SEE WHERE WE ARE BOUND
THERE! QUEEN MAUDLAND, BEYOND THE MARSH AND LAKES

ARE YOU OKAY NURLIN? I KNOW YOU HATE LEAVING THE HILLS
WE WILL BE OUT OF THIS FOREST SOON AND WILL BE ENTERING THE GREAT MARSH, I HAVE NOT BEEN HERE AND KNOW NOT WHAT IT BE LIKE
OH GREAT! I HATE FORESTS BUT I REALLY HATE SWAMPS!

I DON'T
LIKE THIS
PLACE

MISS SHINE!
WHAT ARE
THESE?
WORRY NOT, THEY
ARE JUST GHOSTS,
THEY CAN DO THEE
NO REAL HARM
YOU KNOW,
THAT DOESN'T MAKE
ME FEEL ANY BETTER
AT ALL!

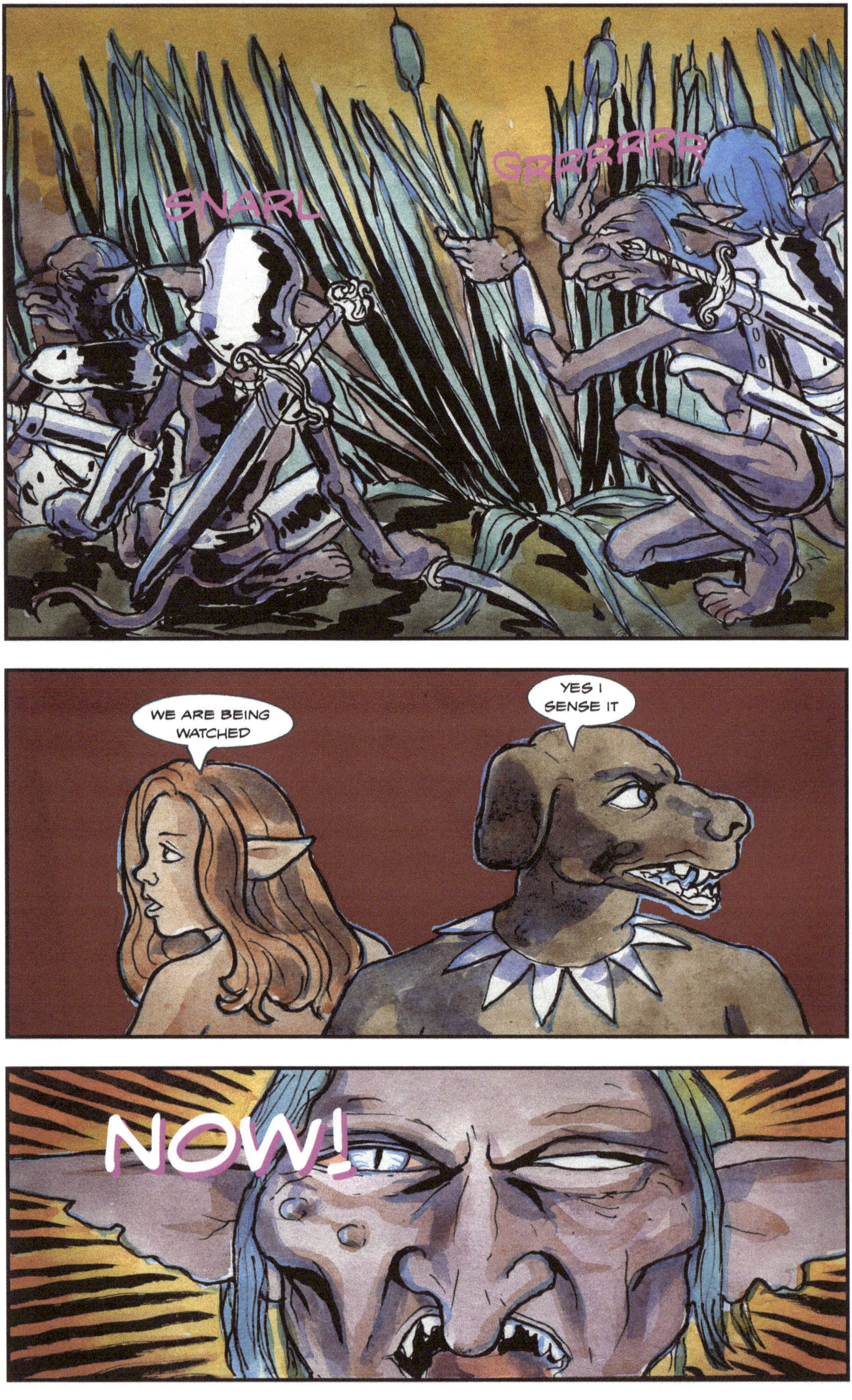

SNARL
GRRRRR

WE ARE BEING WATCHED
YES I SENSE IT

NOW!

STOP THY FIGHTING LITTLE CREATURE, I COULD KILL THEE WITH ONE HAND!
YER NAE SAE TOUGH MOGGIE! KEEK AT YER MUKKERS

WE KIN HAE YER MUKKERS HEIDS AFF IN A MOMENT MOGGIE...
OH, ALL RIGHT, DALE, NURLIN, STOP FIGHTING
GUID WEE PUSS

WHY DOST THOU KEEP CALLING ME CAT, I AM GOBLIN
YER NAY A TRUE GOBLIN, FOLK MADE YE. WE UR GNOMES, WE UR TH' LAST O' TH' REAL FAIRY FOLK

YER NAE REAL FAERIES

REAL OR NAE, AH KEN YER PEOPLE AH BONNIE FIGHTERS

WE AINLIE WAANT PEACE, BIT NOO WE HAE YER MUKKERS TRUSSED UP LIK' A BRACE O' PARTRIDGES YE WULL HULP US

WHAT BOON DOST THOU SEEK?

THERE BE FOLK WHA PREY OAN US, THAY MURDURR 'N' EAT ANY THAY CATCH, MOSTLY OOR BAIRNS. WE HAE TRIED TAE CHASE THAIM AFF BIT THAY MURDURRED MAIST O' OOR WARRIORS, WE UR A' THETS LEFT

THIS SEEMS AN HONOURABLE ENTERPRISE, FREE MY COMPANIONS AND I WILL HELP THEE

NAY, AH WULL KEEP THAIM AS WEE LEVERAGE LES YE CHAYNGE YER MYND

I WILL NOT ARGUE NOW, BUT KNOW THIS, IF THOU HARMEST THEM, I WILL KILL YOU ALL!

AH, THESE BE THY KITS, WORRY NOT LITTLE ONES, I WILL RID THEE OF THESE MEN

BEYOND THE SNOWLINE THEY SAID, NOW WHERE WOULD I HIDE IF I WERE A BAND OF RAGGED MEN... THERE, THAT MOUNTAIN VALLEY, EASY TO DEFEND, GOOD SHELTER...

THERE ARE AROUND 30 OF THEM, SOME MORE MAYMAP IN THE SHEDS

IT IS TRUE, THEY KILL THE GNOMES FOR FOOD

CRACK!

RIPP

CRUNCH
PLEASE..HAVE YOU COME TO RESCUE US?
WHO ART THOU? WHO ARE THESE ROUGH MEN?
THEY CALL THEMSELVES 'THE BROTHERHOOD,' THEY HAVE KEPT US HERE AS THEIR SLAVES... THEY MAIMED US SO WE CAN'T RUN

I KNEW NOT OF THY PLIGHT, BUT YES, I WILL RESCUE THEE
WHEN I HAVE FREED THEE FROM THY DURANCE, FLEE AS FAST AS THOU MAY TO THE NORTH
SNAP!

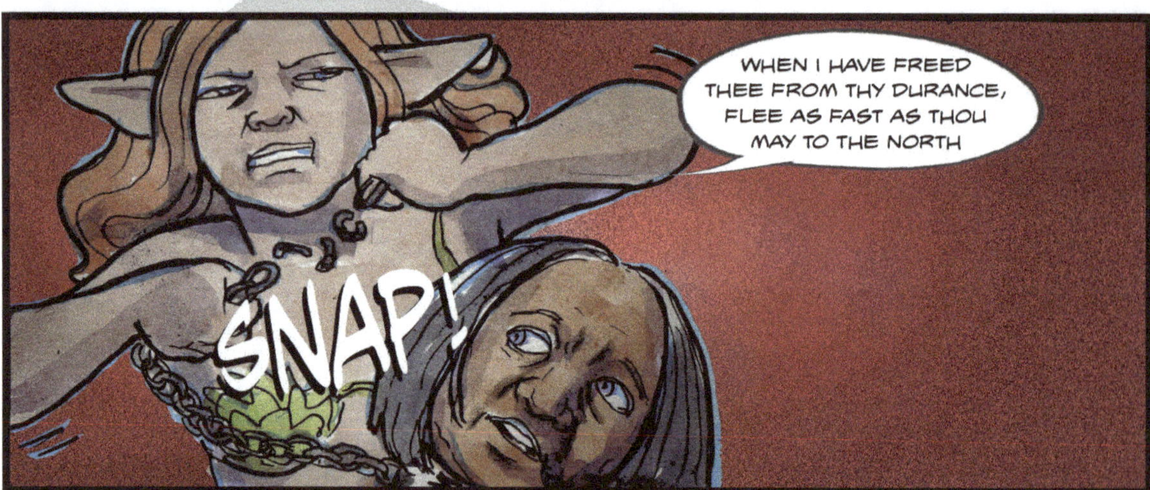

FEAR NOT, I HAVE NEED OF SOME ANGRY DISCOURSE WITH THESE MEN, THEY WILL NOT BE ABLE TO FOLLOW AFTER THEE
TAKE CARE, THEY ARE CUNNING MEN, THEY HAVE MANY TRAPS

GRRRR
CRASH!

I SEE YOU FOUND OUR TRAP GOBLIN, THAT'S GOOD, I WAS GETTING TIRED OF EATING GNOME, LET'S SEE WHAT GOBLIN TASTES LIKE

YOU ARE TRAPPED DOWN THERE GOBLIN, UNTIL WE ARE READY TO KILL AND EAT YOU, IN THE MEANTIME MY BOYS WILL ROUND UP THE WOMEN YOU RELEASED. I PERSONALLY HAMSTRUNG EACH OF THEM SO THEY CANT HAVE GOT TOO FAR

MEEEEEOOOOOWWW

CRUNCH
CRACK
GRRRRRRRR
HIIISSSS-EEEEOOOW

I AM GOBLIN!
AND GOBLIN ARE
NOT PREY

WHAT
ARE
YOU...

THEY MAIMED
THEIR WOMEN, THEY
KILLED AND ATE THE
GNOMES. THEY
HAD TO GO

GNOMES, I AM BACK FOR MY COMPANIONS, I HAVE RID THEE OF THE HUMANS WHO PREYED ON THEE, THY KITS ARE NOW SAFE
THESE FEMALES ARE IN NEED OF THY SUCCOUR, THEY WERE ILL USED BY THE MEN, THEY NEED HEALING AND ALL THY TALENTS AS METAL WRIGHTS TO MAKE THEM AIDS FOR WALKING
AYE, WE KEN THEIR NEED, FEAR NAE MOGGIE, WE'LL CARE FUR THAIM

WE COULD HAVE BROKEN OUT, WE SHOULD HAVE COME WITH YOU TO HELP

THAT'S OKAY, I WAS AFEARD THY STRUGGLES WOULD HARM THE GNOMES

LIKE MANY LITTLE FOLK, THEY WERE NOT AS TOUGH AS THEY BELIEVED
BESIDE, THERE ARE SOME JOBS I AM BETTER TO DO ALONE

MISS SHINE, I DON'T THINK THEY'RE USED TO SEEING PEOPLE LIKE US HERE
GASP!
WE SEEK DISCOURSE WITH THY GOD'S, WHERE SHALL WE FIND THEM?
ARE YOU DJINN?
WHY DO YOU SEEK THEM, IT IS NOT GOOD TO DRAW THE ATTENTION OF GODS
I SEEK A BOON FROM THEM

I THINK YOUR QUEST IS FOOLISH, THE GODS WON'T HELP YOU, BUT YOU'LL FIND THEM IN THEIR GREAT TEMPLE IN THE CITY
THERE SEEM TO BE LOTS OF COWS HERE, THEY MUST EAT LOTS
PERHAPS THEY JUST LIKE COWS
LET US GO, I WILL FIND A GOD TO HELP
I'M HAPPY TO GO ON THIS VOYAGE WITH YOU SHINE, BUT DON'T WORRY IF WE CAN'T GET ME A REAL BODY, IT IS OKAY LIKE THIS

THIS IS LIKE THE LAND OF THE ELDISIL
LET'S HOPE THEY ARE MORE FRIENDLY HERE, THEY TRIED TO KILL US THERE

HEY FREAKS, WHAT ARE YOU DOING HERE?
COME WITH US WE CAN GIVE YOU JOBS IN THE THEATRE
GOOD JOBS, HIGH PAY

NO THANK THEE, WE ARE ON A MISSION, OUR DESTINY LIES ELSEWHERE

GRAB THEM!

HIIISSS
ROOAAAR
CRACK!

WACK!
DALE!
CRUNCH

DRAG THEM TO THE CAGES AND THROW THEM IN
THE ONE THAT WENT OVER THE WALL LOOKS DEAD
LEAVE HIM FOR THE CROWS

WHERE IS DALE, OUR OTHER COMPANION?
GGGRRRR!
THE SILVER FACED FREAK? HE'S DEAD, HE WENT OVER THE WALL
IF HE BE DEAD, I WILL KILL YOU ALL
HIIISSS!
CRACK!
CRACK!
AWAY FROM THE BARS FREAKS!

BE NOT AFEARED NURLIN, I WILL GET US OUT, I CANNOT BEND THE BARS BUT THE CHANCE TO RUN WILL COME
RUSTLE RUSTLE
GASP!

IT'S OKAY SHINE, IT'S JUST ME
DALE! I WAS SO WORRIED, ART THOU HALE?
I HAVE A FEW DENTS BUT I'M OKAY, WHEN I FELL I COULDN'T MOVE,, THEN IT ALL WENT DARK
IT WAS LIKE THIS BODY HAD TO REBOOT, AFTER A WHILE LIGHT AND SOME MOVEMENT CAME BACK
ARE YOU BOTH ALRIGHT? DID THEY HURT YOU? I'M SO SORRY THAT I COULDN'T BE HERE SOONER
I'VE HAD BETTER DAYS ... AND I THINK I WANT TO HIT SOME OF THOSE MEN

WE TRIED BEFORE AND COULD NOT BEND THE BARS, MAYHAP ALL TOGETHER?
CREEEAAAK

OOOF
MIND MY BACK

ROOAAR!
HIIISSS!

LET US MAKE HASTE TO THE GODS TEMPLE, I DESIRE TO BE QUIT OF THIS PLACE

NO, NO YOU CAN'T COME IN HERE!

I LIKE THY CITY LITTLE AND WILL BROOK NO FURTHER DELAYS, I WILL SEE THY GODS NOW!

EXCUSE OUR INTRUSION BUT I SEEK A BOON FROM A GOD, I WANT MY COMPANION DALE MADE HUMAN AGAIN

WHO LET THESE MORTALS IN HERE, WHERE ARE THE MONKS
I ASKED THEE NICELY,, NOW I ASK THEE AGAIN – CAN THOU MAKE DALE HUMAN AGAIN?
WHAT? WHAT DO YOU WANT?

YOU NEED A WORLD CREATING GOD LIKE ZEUS OR JEHOVAH
YOU ARE WASTING YOUR TIME GIRL, NONE OF US CAN DO THAT SORT OF MAGIC
WHERE CAN I FIND ZUES, I FEAR JEHOVAH WILL HELP ME NOT...

HOW DARE YOU COME HERE AND THREATEN MY GODS YOU PUNY MORTALS

YOU WILL ALL DIE FOR YOUR IMPERTINENCE
SPLAT! 
CRUNCH

MISS..SHINE..
I..CAN'T ...MOVE ,OR
BREATHE... I FEEL
I'M BEING SQUASHED
UNDER GLASS

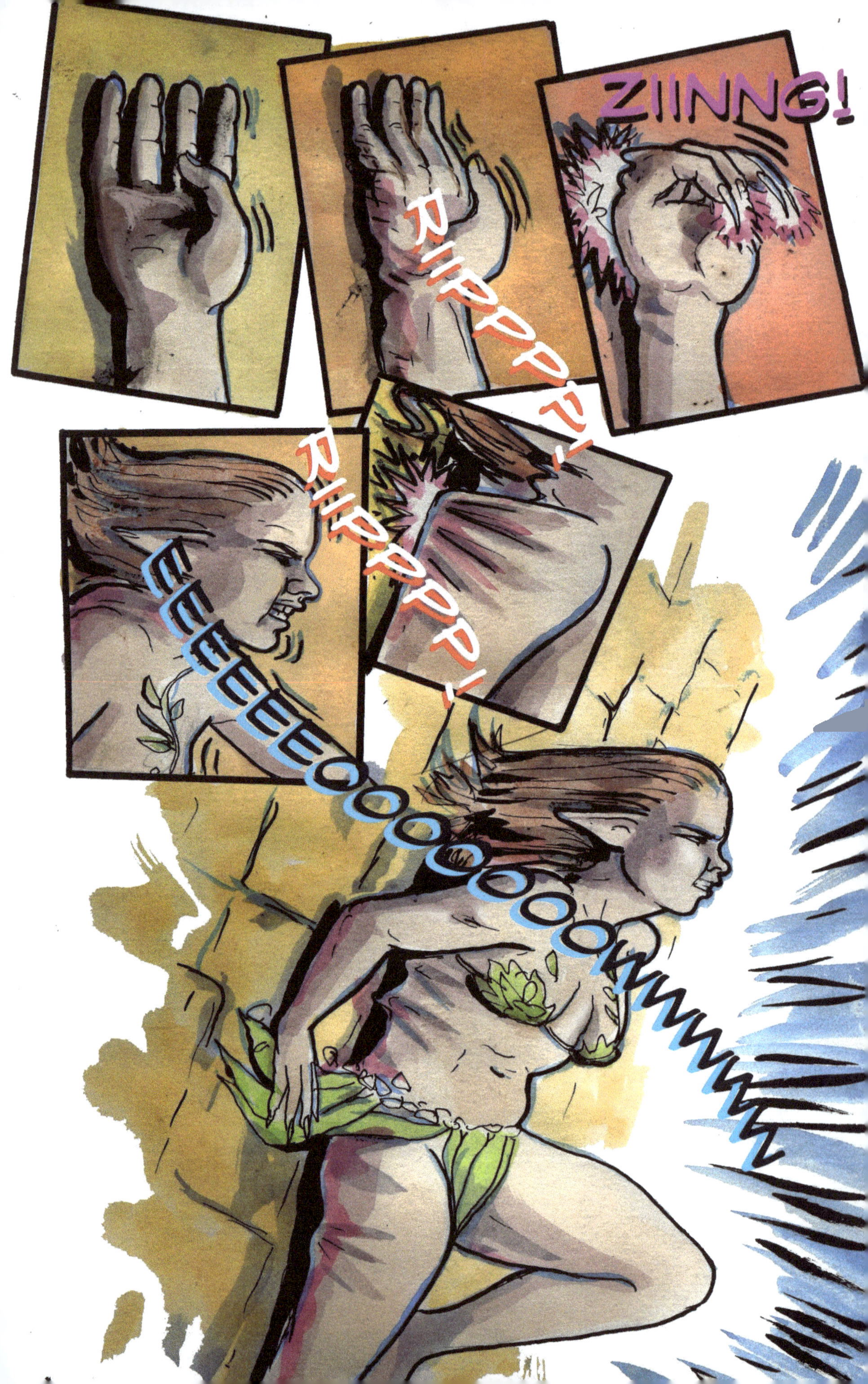

ZIINNG!
RIPPP!
RIPPP!
EEEEEOOOOOOOW!

MEEEOOOOW
RIIIPP!
IF THOU VALUESTS THY EARS THEN LET MY FRIENDS GO, LET THEM LEAVE THIS PLACE

SCREEE - THUMP
DALE AND NURLIN, GO OUTSIDE, I WOULD HAVE DISCOURSE WITH THIS GOD

BOOOM CRASH

IN THE END HE WAS HELPFUL — WE NEED TO FIND ZEUS, HE BIDETH IN A PLACE CALLED OLYMPUS, WE MUST SEEK INGRESS THERE

THE THREE FACED GOD SAID WE NEED TO VISIT NEW IRELAND AND SEEK A PORTAL TO THE GODS REALM
HE SAID WE MUST HASTEN TO THE DOCKS AND TAKE A BOAT

CAN WE TAKE ANY BOAT?
YES, HE JUST SAID TO GET GOING SOON
I SUSPECT HE JUST WANTED TO GET RID OF YOU

BUT WHY WOULD HE WANT TO BE RID OF ME, I DIDN'T ACTUALLT RIP HIS EARS OFF?

MISS SHINE, HOW ARE YOU ABLE TO BEAT UP GODS?

IT'S BECAUSE OF BELIEF, GODS EXIST BECAUSE OF OUR BELIEF, SHINE REALLY BELIEVES, SHE REALLY BELIEVES SHE CAN BEAT UP GODS - SO SHE CAN

MISS SHINE, DO YOU KNOW HOW TO GET TO NEW IRELAND?

NOT REALLY, BUT IF WE KEEP THE MORNING SUN TO OUR LEFT WE WILL GET TO SOMEWHERE

ART THOU SAYING SOME ARE AFFEARED OF ME?
YOU ... CAN BE A LITTLE ... INTIMIDATING MISS SHINE
I THINK I SEE LAND, AN ISLAND PERHAPS
HMMMPH!

UM... YES, LET'S STEER TO IT

I THINK THESE ARE THE LOST ISLANDS
WE LEFT WITHOUT PROVISSIONS, MAYHAP WE CAN ASK THESE PEOPLE FOR SUCCOUR
I WILL ENDEVOUR NOT TO SCARE THEM
OH SHINE, PLEASE LET IT GO

PRAY FRIENDS
WHAT IS THIS
PLACE?

THESE ARE
THE IMPERIAL
ISLANDS,

OOH! WHERE DID YOU COME FROM?

DO NOT SPEAK! MARCH!

AAH, INTERESTING, WE DO NOT SEE MANY FROM THE MAINLAND,, YOU MAY HAVE THE HONOUR OF JOINING OUR SLAVE FORCES

SHINE, NOW'S THE TIME TO BE A LITTLE SCARY

I WILL SAVE THEE BUT I'M A LITTLE AFEARED FOR THY SAFETY

NURLIN CAN LOOK AFTER HERSELF AND I'M PRETTY HARD TO DAMAGE - GO FOR IT

OK - DUCK

WACK
WACK
WACK
WACK

AND NOW
WE DEPART IN
GREAT HASTE

ONCE WE REACH
THE SEA WE CAN
FOLLOW THE SHORE
TO OUR BOAT

RUMBLE RUMBLE

CLANG!
IT'S OKAY, I CAN THROW YOU BOTH TO THE TOP AND YOU CAN PULL ME UP

MAYHAP IF WE
RETREAT BACK INTO
THE TOWN... OH

RUMBLE RUMBLE

SLAM! SLAM! SLAM!

RUMBLE
RUMBLE
HISSSS
HISSSS
WARE, KEEP BEHIND ME

SCREEEECH
ROOOAAAR!

QUICK! GET OUT OF ITS WAY!
ROOOAAARR!
IF THOU KNOWEST WHAT IS GOOD FOR THEE, STAY BACK DRAGON

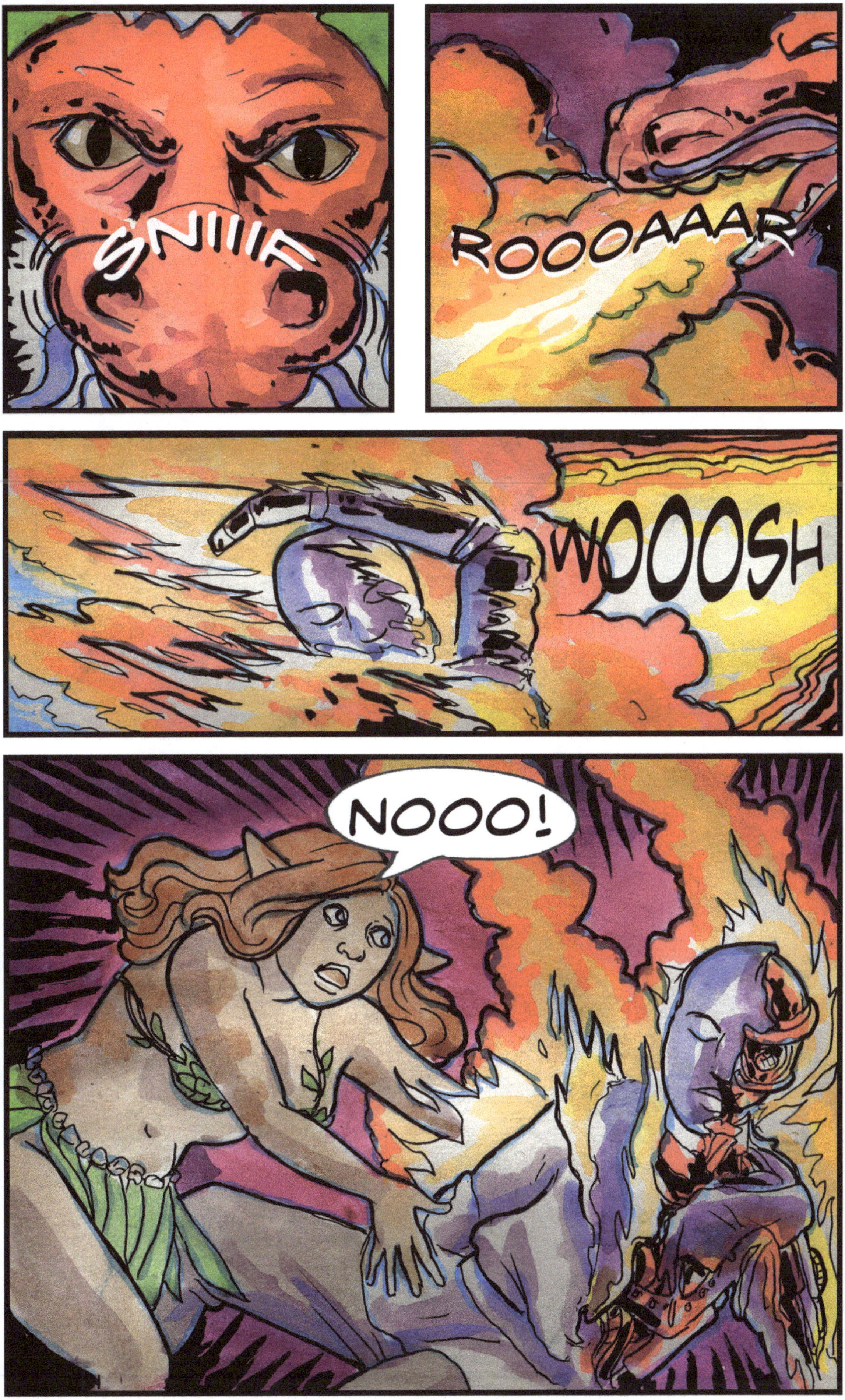

SNIIIF

ROOOAAAR

WOOOSH

NOOO!

ART THOU STILL IN THERE MY LOVE?
YES SHINE, BZZZ, ALTHOUGH -BZZZ- I CAN'T MOVE MY RIGHT ARM...
BZZZ- BZZZ- SHINE-BZZZ, PLEASE DON'T HURT THE DRAGON, THEY ARE SPECIAL CREATURES

HIIISSS!
HIIISSS!

THOU HAST HURT DALE! I SHOULD TEAR THY GIANT HORSEY HEAD FROM THY BODY - BUT DALE HAS PLEADED FOR THY SUCCOUR, SO, LEAVE THIS PLACE ERE I CHANGETH MY MIND

HE'S SHORT CIRCUITING, WE MUST GET HIM OUT OF HERE, USE THY STRENGTH TO OPEN A WAY
CRZZZZ
PZZZ

HOLD ON MY LOVE, WE WILL FIX THEE
PZZZ

MISS SHINE! I CAN OPEN THIS DOOR!
CREEAK

OH DEAR,
UM MISS SHINE?
UM...

AAH... I'LL
JUST CLOSE
THIS DOOR...

CRASH

BZZZK
NURLIN, PRAY TAKE DALE, TRY TO GET AWAY IN THE EXCITMENT AND PLEASE FIX HIM
GREETINGS GIRL, MY NAME IS DAWN LIGHT, THIS IS MY PARTNER, EVENING SHADOW..... I BELIEVE YOU JUST HAD DEALINGS WITH OUR SON, MOUNTAIN MIST
HE LEFT SOME UNFINISHED BUSINESS WITH YOUR GROUP
AND WE WILL FINISH IT!

WE THANK YOU FOR NOT KILLING OUR SON, HE IS YOUNG AND HAS MUCH TO LEARN
DONT GET TOO CLOSE TO A GOBLIN, FOR A START!

HOW CAN WE HELP YOU
WHERE DO YOU WISH TO BE?
WE NEED TO BE OUT OF THIS PLACE FOR A START
WE SEEK TO TRAVEL TO NEW IRELAND

CLIMB ON MY BACK AND I CAN TAKE YOU

NURLIN, ART THOU ABLE TO WORK ON FIXING DALE AS WE ARE FLYING?
THEN YES, THY ASSISTANCE ON OUR QUEST WOULD BE MUCH APPRECIATED
YES, AS LONG AS SHE FLIES STEADY
COME MY LOVE, WE WILL FIX THEE

TAKE CARE
NURLIN, HE WILL
AWAKE WON'T HE?
HE MUST!

HE'S GOING TO LOSE
AN EYE AND AN ARM, AND
HE WON'T BE PRETTY BUT
YES, HE WILL BE OK

BZZK

BZZK

SHINE, I'M SO SORRY TO BE SUCH A PEST, I COULD HEAR BUT COULDN'T MOVE
I'M JUST GLAD THOU ART HALE
I FEEL OK, I CAN MOVE AND SEE AGAIN THANK YOU NURLIN FOR YOUR WORK

WE APPROACH THE ISLAND, I WILL LEAVE YOU NEAR THE MOUNTAINS

THANK YOU DAWN LIGHT, THY GIFT OF TRANSPORT WAS MUCH NEEDED

SHE COULD HAVE LEFT US NEAR THE TOWN
PERHAPS SHE DID NOT DESIRE TO BE SHOT AT, ALSO, SHE KNEW OUR QUEST, WE WILL NOT FIND ASSISTANCE IN TOWN, ALAS BUT, WE NEED DISCOURSE WITH THE DAMNED FAERIES

FAE DOMICILES ARE USUALLY WHERE IT IS HARD TO FIND,, UP HERE LOOKS PROMISING

DON'T WORRY DALE, I'VE GOT YOU

AHH! A FAERIE DELL

COME ON FAERIES, I KEN THOU ART HERE, I NEED THY COUNCEL
OOH LOOK, IT'S THE GOBLIN, HOW FUNNY
AND LOOK, SHE'S GOT HER PETS, THE TROLL AND THE HUMAN
BUT LOOK, THE HUMAN IS ALL BROKEN, HE'S NOT EVEN A REAL BOY ANYMORE, HE'S A BROKEN TOY HA HA HA

HE'S NOT A REAL BOY, JUST A BROKEN LITTLE TOY!
OOH, IT'S SO SAD, SO SAD HA HA HA
OOH, LOOK, HE'S ALL SAD, HE KNOWS HE'S JUST A BURDEN, YOU CARRY HIM AROUND LIKE A BROKEN PUPPET
SUCH A WASTE OF SPACE, JUST A PILE OF OLD METAL, SO SAD
LOOK HOW THE GOBLIN PROTECTS HER TOYS HA HA
BUT YOU WANT OUR HELP, DON'T YOU GOBLIN, YOU WANT TO MAKE HIM A REAL BOY AGAIN!, IT'S SO SWEET HA HA
SO SWEET, SO SWEET HA HA HA
SHUT UP FAERIES!

SNAP
LISTEN THOU HORRIBLE LITTLE THINGS, I WILL TEAR THY WINGS FROM THY BACKS IF THOU HELPETH ME NOT
HA HA! STUPID FAERIES GOT CAUGHT HA HA
WHAT DO YOU WANT UGLY GOBLIN?
WE CAN'T DO THAT EITHER BUT THERE IS ONE WHO IS VISITING THIS REALM FROM DEATHS KINGDOM, SHE COULD HELP YOU
THOU ART RIGHT, I WANT TO HELP DALE BUT I KEN THY MAGIC CAN'T DO THAT SO I SEEK THE WAY TO ZEUS'S HOUSE
YOU WILL FIND HER NORTH IN THE MAGELLAN SWAMPS

THEY ARE REALLY MEAN BUT AT LEAST THEY HELPED IN THE END
THEY WILL DO WHAT THE FIND MOST DIVERTING AND AMUSING, WE HAD BETER STAY WARY
YOU DIDN'T TELL HER OF THE DEARG DUE HA HA HA
HA HA, NO, LET THEM DISCOVER THE VAMPIRES BY THEMSELVES

SHINE, IT'S ALL GETTING TOO MUCH, WE CAN GO HOME I DON'T MIND
NO! WE CAN DO THIS, WE ARE ALMOST THERE NOW, THE SWAMP IS AHEAD

THIS LOOKS LIKE THE START OF THE SWAMP
YES, WE MUST ENTER AND SEARCH

I DON'T LIKE SWAMPS BUT THIS ONE IS'NT TOO BAD

I SMELL BLOOD, THE ODOR OF A CARNIVOR

SCREEECH
SCREEECH

CRUNCH CRUNCH
DON DRAIN AL DEIR BLUD YET, BRIN DEM BACK TER DE VILLAGE OI SAW TREE AV DEM BUT OI CAN SMAEL NAW OTHER LIVIN TIN, LET US GO

COME
SISTERS

HANG ON
SHINE, I'M
COMING

PSST... SHINE ARE YOU ALIVE
SHHH... I SEEK TO PUT THEM AT EASE

EEEEE
NURLIN, I CAN NOT BREAK THESE BONDS!
IT'S OK SHINE RELAX AND I'LL TRY TO UNTIE YOU BOTH
DALE! THOU ART HERE, RUN, LEST THEY CATCH THEE
NO SHINE, I WILL HELP YOU ESCAPE THIS TIME!
OH, SHIT
AAAH, LUK, TIS DE TURD MEMBER AV DIS APPY TROOP. KEEL UT SISTERS

WHAT BE LIT WIVES? IT DOESN'T SMAELL ALOIVE BUT LIT SEEMS ALOIVE, WHY?
SISTERS, LET'S KEEL LIT, OIM STAARVIN
GRRRRR
SNARL
WELL COME ON YOU LOT, TRY BITING ME! YOU'LL GET A SUPRISE

MEEEOOOW
CRUNCH
WACK
THUMP

MISS SHINE! I'M FREE! LET ME HELP!
CRUNCH!
ROOAAR!

GOOD, THEY ARE RUNNING OFF AT LAST
YET WE ARE NO CLOSER IN OUR QUEST FOR ZEUS

SHINE, COME HERE QUICKLY

HELLO SHINE OF THE MOON, AT LEAST I'M IN YOUR TIME

MICHELLE! THOU ART HERE? I SAW YOU LAST IN DEATH'S WORLD, YOU DECIDED TO STAY THERE WITH MY DEAD COUSIN

HOLD STILL, I'LL GET YOU DOWN

THANKYOU MISS TROLL..... SHINE, I WAS TRYING TO COME SEE YOU
YOUR COUSIN, SUN ON THE FOREST FINALLY FADED AWAY, HE HAS GONE ON TO BE REBORN. THE WITCH SAYS HE WILL BE BACK IN A NEW LIFE
I'M SO SORRY, ART THOU AT PEACE WITH THIS, DIDST THOU HAVE LONG WITH HIM?
NOT LONG ENOUGH, I MISS HIM STILL YET IT HAS BEEN A YEAR SINCE HE LEFT, IN DEATHS WORLD IT IS HARD TO TELL TIME, IT FELT LIKE WE HAD YEARS AND JUST DAYS AT THE SAME TIME

THE FAERIES SAID THOU HAST THE GIFT OF MOVING THROUGH THE REALMS, I HATE TO ASK THEE NOW BUT I NEED TO GET DALE TO ZEUS AT OLYMPUS, HE CAN GIVE DALE BACK HIS LIFE, HIS SOUL IS IN THIS TINMAN
YES, I CAN SEND YOU THERE, BUT ....
WAIT, IF YOU CAN DO THAT FOR DALE, I COULD HAVE DONE THIS TO SAVE SUN
YOU KNEW THIS AND DIDN'T TELL ME? ... WHY?
WHY SHOULD I HELP YOU! YOU LET SUN DIE!
I'M SO SORRY, I THOUGHT OF IT NOT, I THOUGHT THOU WERE CONTENT WITH THY BARGAIN WITH DEATH, I NEED THY HELP, I KNOW OF NO OTHER WAY TO GET TO ZEUS...
WELL! YOU HAD BETTER FIND ANOTHER WAY... BECAUSE I'LL NOT HELP YOU!
BLIP

THIS IS YOUR PROBLEM, YOU ALWAYS FEEL YOU SHOULD SAVE EVERYONE
I WILL FIND A WAY TO ZEUS, I WILL SAVE THEE DALE BUT NOW I FEEL BAD I COULD NOT SAVE SUN ON THE FOREST
IT'S OK SHINE, I'M STILL HERE, THIS BODY IS ALRIGHT

BLIP!

DAMN YOU SHINE OF THE MOON! I KNOW IT'S NOT REALLY YOUR FAULT...

I'VE BEEN STUDYING WITCHCRAFT BUT IT NEVER OCCURED TO ME TO TRY TO FIND A WAY HE COULD STAY

I DIDN'T REALLY BELIEVE HE'D DIE, I JUST THOUGHT HE'D ALWAYS BE THERE SOB
HAVE FAITH MICHELLE, I KNOW MY COUSIN, HE'LL FIND A WAY BACK!

I WILL SEND YOU TO MOUNT OLYMPUS, BUT IT WILL BE NOT EASY TO GET THE GODS TO HELP
I THANK THEE MICHELLE
STAND VERY CLOSE TOGETHER

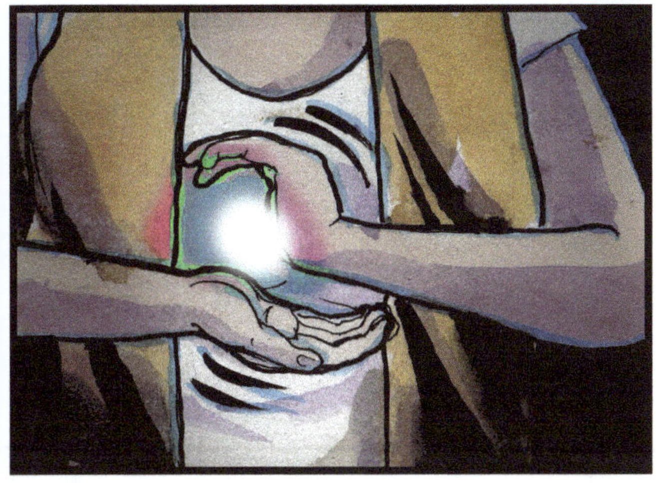

BLIP!

WHERE ARE WE MISS SHINE?
MIHELLE CALLED THIS MOUNT OLYMPUS SO WE WALK UP THE SLOPE
THERE- IT IS A MOUNTAIN, WE PROCEED UP

RUMBLE
RUMBLE
RUMBLE
SOMETHING IS COMING

WHEEE
AARRG
RUMBLE
RUMBLE
RUMBLE

GREETINGS HORSE PEOPLE, WE SEEK A MEETING WITH ZEUS
HIC YOU DOAN WAN TU TALK WI ZEUS, HE'S THE BOSS, *HIC* YOU MORTALS, HOW YOU GET HERE ANY... ANYWAY *HIC*

PRAPS ZEUS MII LIKE YOU, HE *HIC* LIKES MORTAL GIRLS *HIC* SMTIMES
THIS ONE'S AN AUTOMATUM, LIKE KING PYGMALION TRIED TO MAKE, CAN I PULL ITS HEAD OFF AN KEEP IT? UTS PREETY AN SHINY

MEEEEEE

CRUNCH

HISSSSS

IF THOU HURTS DALE I WILL BREAK THY NECK THEN TEAR THY HEAD FROM THY FAT DONKEY BODY
CRUNCH

CRUNCH

GLUG GLUG
I WUZ WRONG, ZEUS WDN'T LIKE HER, IF HE TRIED HUS TRICKS WUTH HER *HIC* SHE PROBABLY KICK HIM IN THE THROAT

JUS TAKE EM TO DU EDGE AN CHUCK EM OFF

OVER YOU GO, SAY HELLO TO THE HARPIES AS YOU GO PAST, HA HA

DALE, I'M GOING TO GRAB YOUR ARM
NOW I'LL GRAB SHINE OF THE MOON
MISS SHINE MISS SHINE, ARE YOU DEAD?
OOOOH... NOT QUITE

OKAY, I'VE WORKED OUT HOW TO DIRECT OUR FALL FLIGHT, I MOVE US OVER TO THE CLIFF AND GRAB A ROCK, I'M SURE I'M STRONG ENOUGH FOR IT TO WORK

IT IS A STRONG AND BRAVE PLAN AND MAY HAVE BEEN POSSIBLE, BUT THERE IS A FLAW, CAST THY EYES UP

OH SHIT, THE WHOLE MOUNTAIN IS FLOATING , HOW? AND WE'RE BELOW BUT THERES NO GROUND UNDER US EITHER

SOME BIG BIRDS FLY YONDER, THEY SEEM TO BE COMING TO US, IF I CAN CAPTURE ONE IT MAY FLY US TO SAFETY

SCREECH
OH, BIG GRUMPY BIRD LADIES, THE PLAN REMAINS THE SAME

DALE, NURLIN, HOLD ON TIGHT TO EACH OTHER
EEEOOOW
SCREEEECH
I HOPE THOU KENS MY WORDS BIRD LADY, I NEED THEE TO CATCH MY FRIENDS IN THY TALONS AND CARRY US ALL TO THE PEAK OF YON MOUNTAIN
i understand you well enough prey, why would i do this?

SIGH, I TIRE OF UNHELPFUL PEOPLE, IF THOU HELP ME NOT I WILL TEAR OPEN THY THROAT AND REACH INTO THY CHEST AND SQUEEZE THY HEART UNTILL THOU DOST!
oh, okay

ARE WE ALL HALE?
NO, I DON'T THINK MY STOMACH LIKES THIS FLYING
I;M SORRY NURLIN BUT LET US GO AND VISIT THESE GODS

GO AWAY! SHOO!

YOU CAN'T COME IN HERE, MORTALS CAN'T COME IN!

I WISH
TO BE TAKEN
BEFORE ZEUS

WHY? WHAT
DO YOU WANT
HIM TO DO?

I HAVE HEARD HE IS
THE ONLY GOD WHO CAN
TURN DALE INTO A REAL
HUMAN AGAIN

WHY DO YOU THINK HE WILL HELP YOU?

I HAVE BEEN TOLD HE IS A MIGHTY GOD AND COULD EASILY DO THIS, SO WHY WOULD HE NOT? I WILL APPEAL TO HIS HEART

HA HA HA HA

WE WILL TAKE YOU BEFORE ZEUS, WE WANT TO WATCH
BEHOLD, THE GREAT GOD ZEUS

GREAT ZEUS, I SEEK A BOON FROM THEE. THIS IS MY LOVED PARTNER DALE. TWICE I HAVE HAD TO BRING HIM BACK FROM DEATH'S REALM. THIS TIME HIS BODY HAD BEEN DESTROYED AND WE HAD TO PLACE HIS SOUL IN THIS TINMAN...
I NEED HIM TO BE HUMAN AGAIN, LIVING AS AN AUTOMATUM IS NOT REALLY LIVING, I BROUGHT HIM BACK FROM DEATH FOR MYSELF— NOW I NEED TO DO THIS FOR HIM

I HAVE THE POWER TO DO THIS, I COULD DO IT WITH A CLICK OF MY FINGERS, BUT WHY SHOULD I?
I GET NOTHING FROM THIS TRANSACTION, YOU CAN OFFER ME NOTHING, I DO NOT WISH TO BREED WITH YOU, MY CENTAURS TOLD ME ABOUT YOU AND YOU ARE NOT COMPLIENT ENOUGH TO INTEREST ME
NO, I WILL NOT HELP YOU, TAKE THEM AWAY

HISSSS
I WAS HOPING TO APPEAL TO THY HEART, BUT ALAS, THY HEART IS DRY AND COLD
I WILL GET THY HELP OR I WILL OPEN THY WORTHLESS THROAT!
BOOOM!

HA HA HA HA
YOU HAVE COURAGE, AT LEAST YOU HAVE AMUSED ME THIS DAY, I WILL RESTORE YOUR BOY, I WILL MAKE HIM HUMAN AND JUST AS YOU BROUGHT HIM
CLICK
WOOF
HELLO SHINE, YOU BROUGHT ME BACK!
THE END - FOR NOW